D0578631

JPIC Whelan
Whelan, Gloria
Mackinac Bridge : the story of th
five-mile poem /   : the story
                                    iile poem

34028073179336
KW $17.95   ocm64390371 $17.95
              05/14/10   ocm64390371
1st ed DISCARD   01/26/2010

Mackinac Bridge

The Story of the Five-Mile Poem

Gloria Whelan - *Illustrated by* Gijsbert van Frankenhuyzen

The Bridge at Mackinac

By David B. Steinman

In the land of Hiawatha,
Where the white man gazed with awe
At a paradise divided
By the straits of Mackinac.

Men are dredging, drilling, blasting,
Battling tides around the clock,
Through the depths of icy water,
Driving caissons down to rock.

Fleets of freighters bring their cargoes
From the forges and the kilns;
Stones and steel—ten thousand barge-loads—
From the quarries, mines, and mills.

Now the towers, mounting skyward,
Reach the heights of airy space.
Hear the rivet-hammers ringing,
Joining steel in strength and grace.

High above the swirling currents,
Parabolic strands are strung;
From the cables, packed with power,
Wonder-spans of steel are hung.

Generations dreamed the crossing;
Doubters shook their heads in scorn.
Brave men vowed that they would build it—
From their faith a bridge was born.

There it spans the miles of water,
Speeding millions on their way—
Bridge of vision, hope and courage,
Portal to a brighter day.

To Connor Nolan

—Gloria

My father was one of those hunters who waited, sometimes all night, to take the ferry from the Lower to the Upper Peninsula of Michigan. As a child I remember taking a ferry when I made my first visit to the three stars of the Upper Peninsula: the Tahquamenon Falls, the Pictured Rocks, and Copper Harbor.

Living only an hour from the straits, I watched, month by month, and year by year, the building of the bridge. I've made many trips across the Mackinac Bridge (and so have characters in my books) but I always catch my breath at the first sight of the stately towers rising in the distance. The bridge is certainly David B. Steinman's finest poem.

— Gloria Whelan

If only his father, Captain Hansen, hadn't been so sad, Mark Hansen's thirteenth summer would have been the happiest summer of his life. Mark's dad was letting him help to line up the cars as they drove onto the *Aurora*.

His dad was captain of a ferryboat that carried travelers across the Straits of Mackinac. This would be the *Aurora*'s last year on the straits.

Mark had been riding the *Aurora* as long as he could remember. On hot summer days Mark had sold lemonade to the long lines of drivers waiting to ride the ferry.

In November deer hunters by the hundreds of thousands traveled to the Upper Peninsula. Mark sold hot chocolate to the hunters, who sometimes had to wait overnight to get onto one of the ferries.

The *Aurora* was the smallest in a fleet of ferries carrying cars and passengers between Mackinaw City and St. Ignace. The ferryboats were like a road on the water connecting Michigan's Upper and Lower Peninsulas. From the deck of the *Aurora* Mark could see what made him so happy and what made his father, Captain Hansen, so sad. He could see the bridge.

When it was finished in the fall the bridge would be the longest bridge in the world. It would stretch an amazing five miles across the Straits of Mackinac.

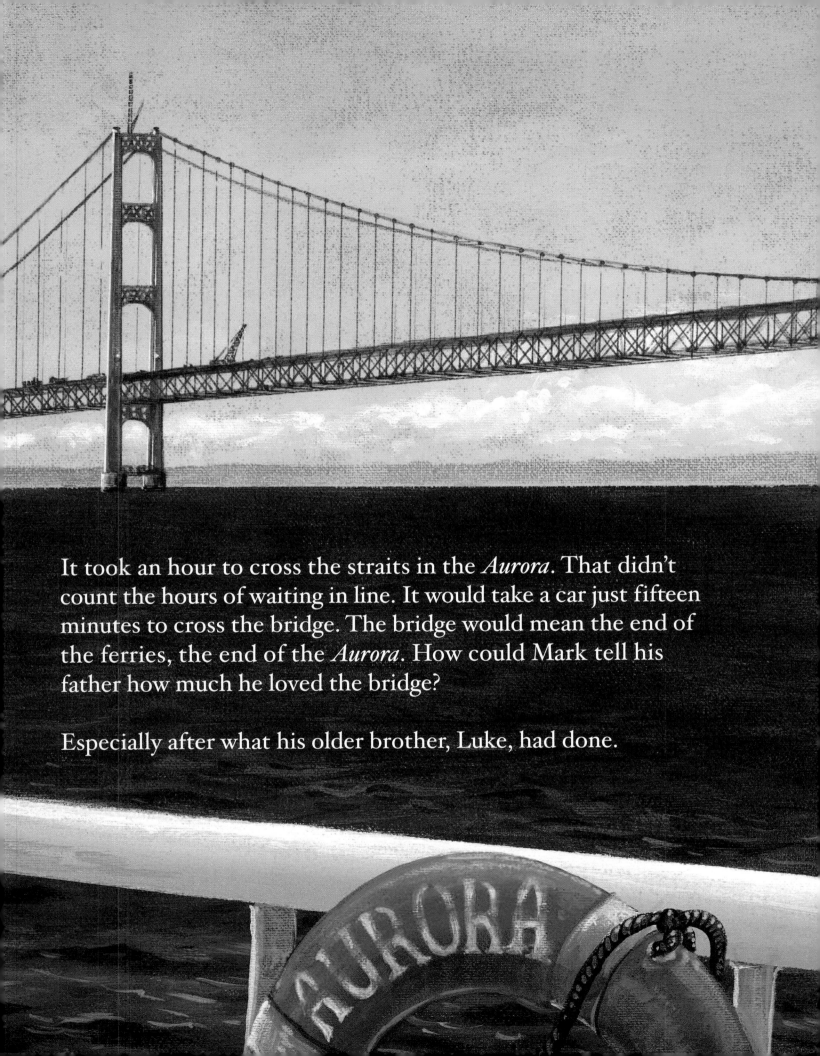

It took an hour to cross the straits in the *Aurora*. That didn't count the hours of waiting in line. It would take a car just fifteen minutes to cross the bridge. The bridge would mean the end of the ferries, the end of the *Aurora*. How could Mark tell his father how much he loved the bridge?

Especially after what his older brother, Luke, had done.

Mark was as proud of the *Aurora* as his dad was. He liked the way the gangplank clanged down with a growl. He liked the way the big mouth of the ferry swallowed up the cars. He liked the *Aurora*, but he loved the idea of a bridge, something that could go right through the air and bring things together.

Mark had heard his father say, "Any bridge across the straits is sure to collapse. It will never hold up to 70-mile-an-hour winds and pounding from ice floes as tall as a 30-foot building." A lot of people shook their heads and said it couldn't be done.

Three years before, in 1954, when they had first begun to build the bridge it looked like all the barges and derricks in the whole world were right out there in the lake.

Luke said, "There's a lot you can't even see. Divers are working hundreds of feet under the water putting in piers to anchor the bridge. Two of the piers are like empty buildings. Two are like giant steel cans. They're going to fill the piers with concrete. Those big barges out there are mixing the concrete, nearly a million tons of the stuff. When the bridge is done, two-thirds of it will be underwater."

Then Luke said something strange. "It's next year I'm waiting for."

"What do you mean?" Mark asked.

"Wait and see," Luke said.

All summer the barges made concrete. All summer the concrete disappeared under the straits. Mark tried to imagine the divers down there with all their equipment. It must be like an under-water city, he thought.

He wished he were there.

When winter came the gulls flew south. Bridge workers left. Ferries stopped their runs. Four feet of ice sealed off the straits. The winds blew and the snow came down and Mark thought about the underwater city beneath the ice.

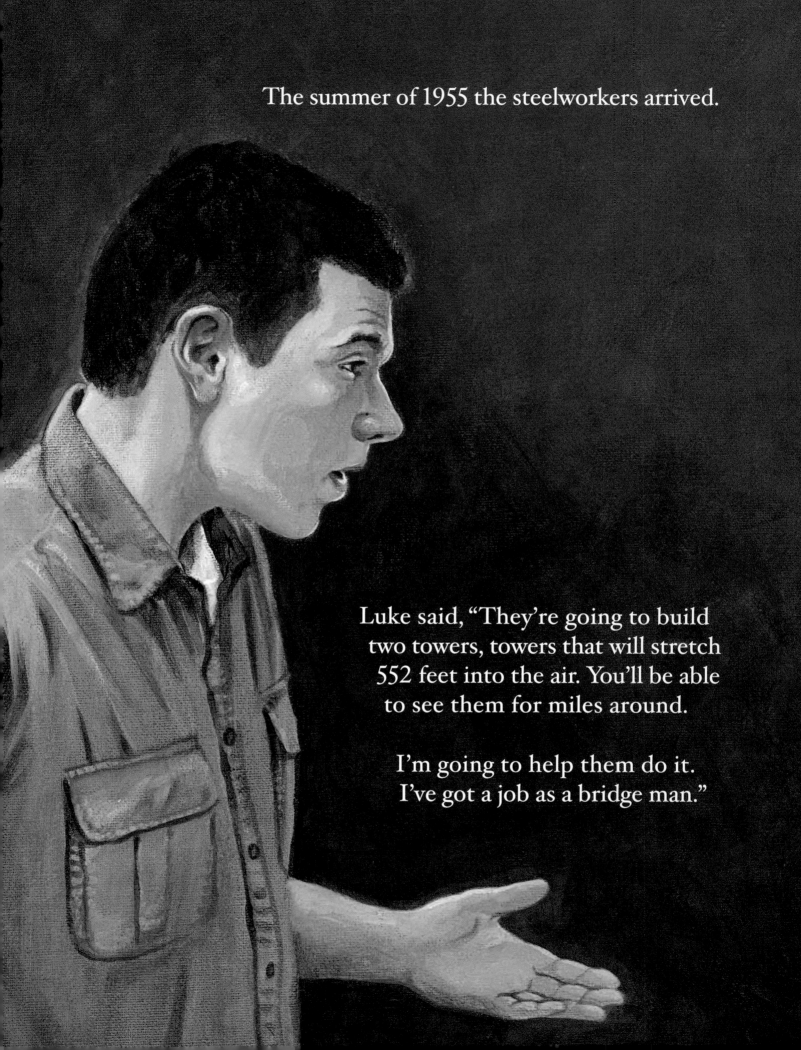

The summer of 1955 the steelworkers arrived.

Luke said, "They're going to build two towers, towers that will stretch 552 feet into the air. You'll be able to see them for miles around.

I'm going to help them do it. I've got a job as a bridge man."

"That bridge is going to put me and the *Aurora* out of business," Captain Hansen said. "How could you give them a hand?"

He stopped talking to Luke. Mealtimes were pretty quiet.

Finally Mrs. Hansen said, "I'm not sitting through another silent dinner. I understand why your dad resents the bridge, but that bridge is going up and Luke might just as well be a part of it."

Captain Hansen said, "Pass the bread, Luke."

The silence was broken. Mark breathed a sigh of relief. He smiled, thinking his mom had been like a bridge herself, bringing his dad and Luke together.

Luke had a special pair of gloves and a helmet to wear at work. He left each morning before Mark was awake.

Mark watched the tower going up on the north side of the bridge. Luke was up on that tower, king of everything he saw. When the first tower was in place, an American flag was hoisted to the top. By October flags were flying on both towers.

In January winter winds lashed the towers, pounding and shaking them. The towers stood firm. With their ice-coated ribs, Mark thought they looked like two frozen skeletons.

Mark and Luke built their own bridge on the kitchen table. "It'll be a suspension bridge," Luke said. "The roadway the cars drive over will be held up by a cradle of cables."

Mark made two towers from milk cartons. "There's nothing in the middle," he said. "How are they going to get the cables from the one tower to the other?"

Luke said, "They'll build a catwalk, a temporary path to walk on while they spin the wires."

Luke wrapped strands of wire around two of their mother's spools of thread. He told Mark to string wire from one end of the bridge to the towers and then to the other end of the bridge. More wires hung down to hold up a cardboard roadway.

They had made a bridge.

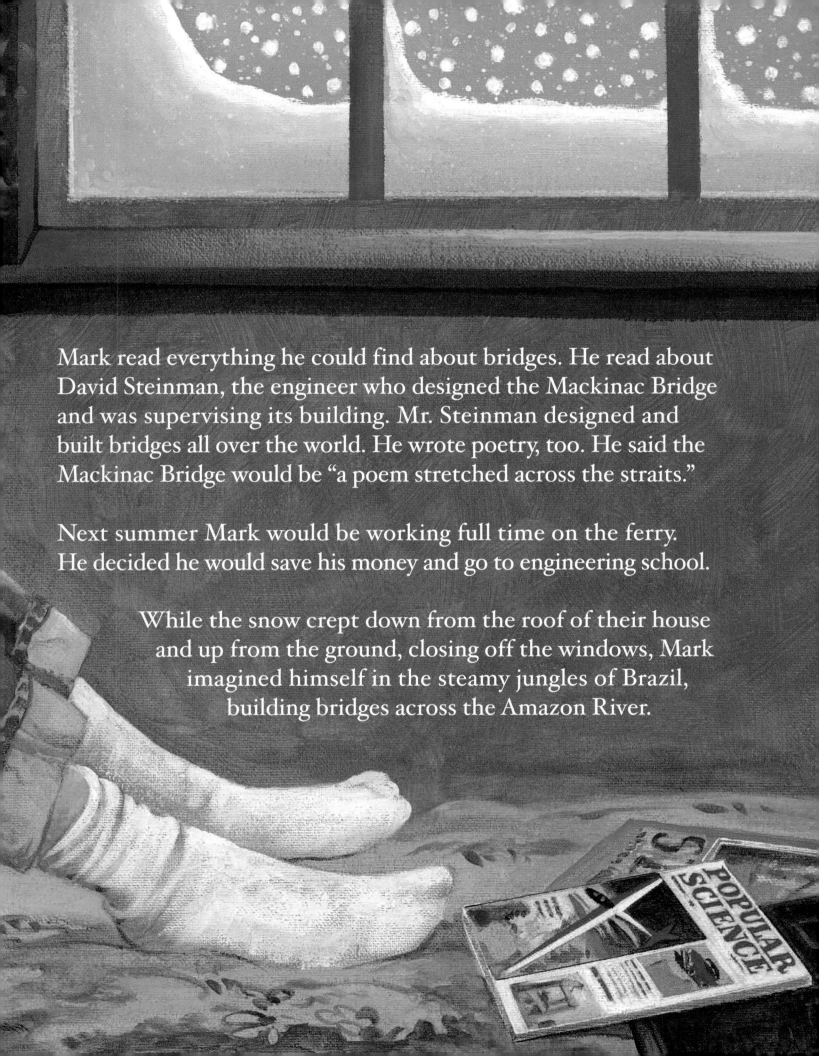

Mark read everything he could find about bridges. He read about David Steinman, the engineer who designed the Mackinac Bridge and was supervising its building. Mr. Steinman designed and built bridges all over the world. He wrote poetry, too. He said the Mackinac Bridge would be "a poem stretched across the straits."

Next summer Mark would be working full time on the ferry. He decided he would save his money and go to engineering school.

While the snow crept down from the roof of their house and up from the ground, closing off the windows, Mark imagined himself in the steamy jungles of Brazil, building bridges across the Amazon River.

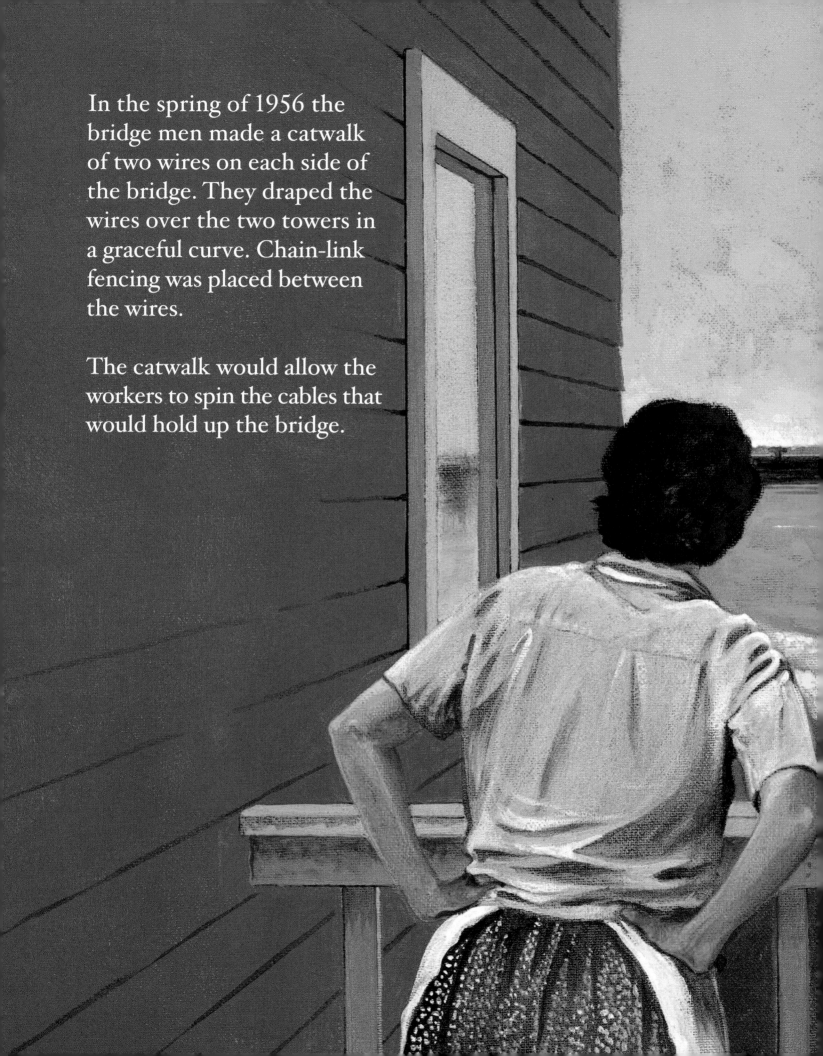

In the spring of 1956 the bridge men made a catwalk of two wires on each side of the bridge. They draped the wires over the two towers in a graceful curve. Chain-link fencing was placed between the wires.

The catwalk would allow the workers to spin the cables that would hold up the bridge.

Luke came home. "I walked it!" he shouted. "I walked right across the bridge on the catwalk."

Mark saw his mom shiver as she looked out at the narrow pathway 500 feet in the air.

"I guess it's time for me to look for a new job," Captain Hansen said.

A necklace of lights was strung along the catwalk for the
bridge men who were working around the clock.

Mark dreamed he was alone up on the catwalk, so close
to the moon and the stars he could touch them.

All summer long, wheels like giant spiders crept back and forth across the bridge stringing wires. Mark could hear the cowbells on the wheels warning the men on the catwalk to get out of the way. There were over 12,000 strands of wire in each cable! The cables had to be strong for they would hold up the floor of the bridge.

Captain Hansen said, "I heard they're going to chop the top off one of the ferries and use it as a barge. I'd sink the *Aurora* before I'd let them do that to her."

That winter an offer came for the ferry. When the bridge was completed the *Aurora* would be sent downstate to the Detroit River. "At least it will still be carrying cars," the captain said.

"What about you, Dad?" Mark asked. "What will you do?"

"I got a pretty good offer from a company whose ferries go from Mackinaw City to Mackinac Island."

"That's great, Dad," Mark said, but he couldn't help thinking of how small those Mackinac Island ferries were. You could put a couple of them inside the *Aurora*.

The April of 1957 brought one of the strait's worst storms. Seventy-mile-an-hour gusts bent the trees and stacked ice as high as skyscrapers.

When the gulls returned later in the spring, the bridge still stood.

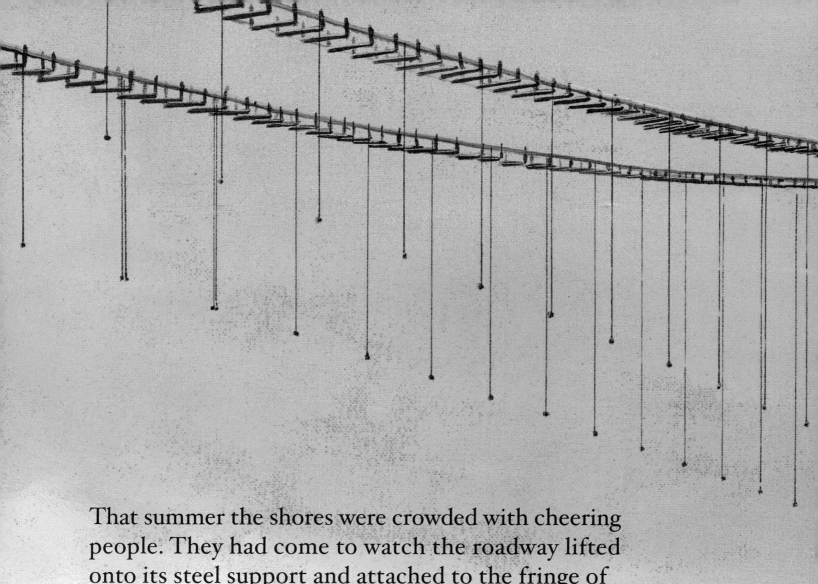

That summer the shores were crowded with cheering people. They had come to watch the roadway lifted onto its steel support and attached to the fringe of wire that hung down from the cables.

At last the Lower and Upper Peninsulas were joined! Mark's heart was going so fast he could hardly breathe.

There was still a lot to do to meet the November 1 deadline. The roadway had to be paved and the bridge painted. Now when Luke went to work, their mom packed dinner for him as well as lunch. Sometimes he didn't get home until midnight.

Sometimes he worked all night.

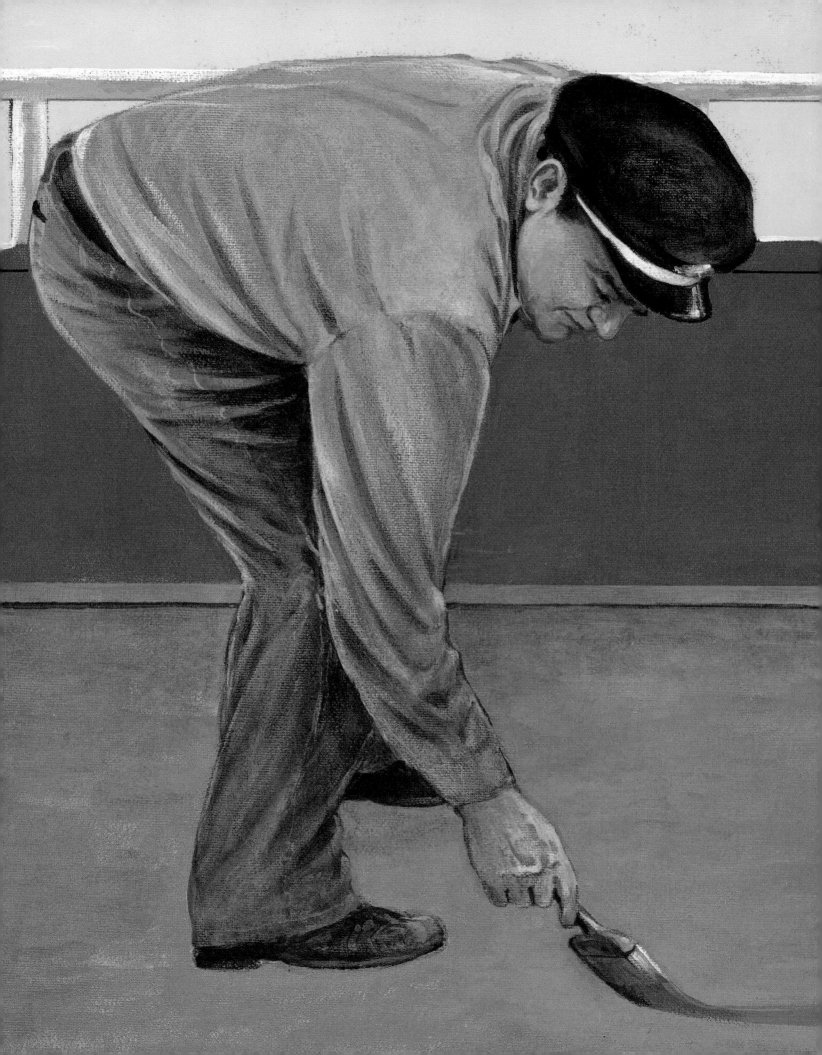

Captain Hansen was working long hours as well.
He was polishing all the bright work on the *Aurora*
and giving her deck a new coat of paint.

"I want to be proud of the boat I send
downstate," he said. He gave the
ferry a loving pat.

Mark jumped out of bed. It was the first of November. Today the bridge would be opened to traffic. Michigan's governor was going to lead the parade. Schools had been given the day off. Hundreds of cars would be crossing the bridge.

Just as Mark and Luke were leaving, the captain said, "I hope you're not planning to cross that bridge without your mother and me."

That night there was a celebration with fireworks. Mark and Luke and their mom and dad watched from the deck of the *Aurora*. The sparks from the fireworks tangled with the lights from the bridge. When the fireworks were over, Captain Hansen brought the ferryboat home from its last trip on the straits.

Later, after everyone was asleep, Mark crept out of the house. It was warm for November. He walked the mile from their house to the straits. The string of lights glittered on the deserted bridge.

Mark was sure that somewhere there was a river wider than the straits and he would build the bridge that crossed it.

A Note from the Mackinac Bridge Authority

The Straits of Mackinac was an apparently insolvable geographical problem—a barrier of deep and turbulent water which cut the state of Michigan in half. The four miles of deep water between Mackinaw City and St. Ignace choked off commerce and culture.

The Mackinac Bridge was built in the face of discouragement, of faintheartedness on the part of many of the state's leaders, of warnings that the rocks in the straits were too soft, the ice too thick, the winds too strong, the rates of interest on the financial bonds too high, and the whole concept too big. Overcoming these obstacles would dictate how the bridge would be designed.

At the time the Mackinac Bridge was built and until 1998, it was the longest suspension bridge in the world. With its official opening on November 1, 1957, one era was ended and another begun. The story of the Mighty Mac is one that combines history, a remarkable engineering achievement, and a work of art.

The Ferryboats

In 34 years of service, the ferries operated by the Department of State Highways carried some 12 million vehicles and more than 30 million passengers across the Straits of Mackinac. The state ferry operation was the only service of its kind operated by a state highway department. It was created due to public displeasure with the expensive, infrequent ferry service for motor vehicles provided by the railroad boats. When the bridge opened in 1957, the ferries stopped (rail boats continued). There were 400 state employees that worked on the boats or on the docks. Some were placed elsewhere in the highway department, while others left their employment in order to remain in the straits area.

Mac Facts

- There are 42,000 miles of wire in the main cables.
- The whole bridge weighs 1,024,500 tons.
- There are almost 5 million rivets in the bridge (4,851,700).

For more information about the Mackinac Bridge Authority,
please visit their Web site at mackinacbridge.org.

—————————— ACKNOWLEDGMENTS ——————————

Sleeping Bear Press wishes to thank and acknowledge Kim Nowack, chief engineer of the Mackinac Bridge Authority, for reading and reviewing the manuscript.

The poem, "The Bridge at Mackinac," by David Steinman has been reprinted with permission from the family of David Steinman.

—

Much appreciation goes to Richard DeMara, one of the original bridge workers, for sharing your home and bridge stories with me. Thanks to Nancy and Dick Campbell for opening your doors to a stranger and sharing your stories, and lending me your Mackinac Bridge helmet and construction photos. You are trusting souls. Many thanks to Bill Phillips from Michigan Dept. of Transportation, who searched the photo archives numerous times to help me find construction photographs taken by Ellis and Bell. Thanks to Ernie Fox, for arranging several meetings with the "1950s car guys." Thanks to Ed Remaly, who hooked me up with Jerry and Marita Archer, who took the time to take me right under the bridge on their sailboat. You were all an invaluable resource.

Finally, thanks to my models, Jake LeuVoy, Jeff Dempsey, and Steve Darling; without you I could not have done the book. —*Gijsbert*

Text Copyright © 2006 Gloria Whelan
Illustration Copyright © 2006 Gijsbert van Frankenhuyzen

All rights reserved. No part of this book may be reproduced in any manner without the express written consent of the publisher, except in the case of brief excerpts in critical reviews and articles. All inquiries should be addressed to:

Sleeping Bear Press™

310 North Main Street, Suite 300
Chelsea, MI 48118
www.sleepingbearpress.com

© 2006 Sleeping Bear Press is an imprint of The Gale Group, Inc.

Printed and bound in China.

First Edition

10 9 8 7 6 5 4 3 2

Library of Congress Cataloging-in-Publication Data

Whelan, Gloria.
Mackinac Bridge : the story of the five-mile poem / written by Gloria Whelan; illustrated by Gijsbert van Frankenhuyzen.
p. cm.
living running a ferry boat, thirteen-year-old Mark and his brother Luke are excited about the building of a five-mile bridge across the Straits of Mackinac in Michigan in 1957.

ISBN 978-1-58536-283-7

1. Mackinac Bridge (Mich.)—Juvenile fiction. [1. Mackinac Bridge (Mich.)—Fiction. 2. Bridges—Design and construction—Fiction. 3. Fathers and sons—Fiction. 4. Michigan—History—20th century—Fiction.] I. Frankenhuyzen, Gijsbert van, ill. II. Title.

PZ7.W5718Mac 2006
[Fic]—dc22   2006001425